Arnie's Christmas Tail

By
Lucy Varga-Sharples

Illustrated By
Enrica Nicola

For my niece, Evelyn Grace

In Loving Memory of Arnie

It was the night before Christmas and all through the town, not a creature was stirring, not even a hound!

The stockings were hung by the chimney with care, but Arnie the Boston terrier wasn't there

The children were nestled all snug in their bed, whilst Arnie was trembling in an old damp shed

He was hungry and cold and all on his own, desperately wishing for a nice warm home

Huddled in a ball, he huffed and sighed, as others rejoiced, and ate mince pies

Arnie could muster no festive cheer, on this most magical day of the year

Then out on the lawn there rose such
a clatter, Arnie leapt from the shed
to see what was the matter

But out on his porch he saw to his fright, a fierce
old Tom cat ready for a fight!

He stood up and stared frozen in place, confronted
by the cat with a mean look on its face!

At the sight this foe, Arnie began to quiver, and
down his spine ran an ice-cold shiver

He had a menacing stare and a battle torn ear;
his presence commanding the toughest dog's fear!

How Arnie tried his best to be courageous, but
that fierce old tom cat was far to audacious!

Screaming and hissing, his claws
in the air, it was far too much
for Arnie to bare.

So, into the woods he ran with haste, in fear for his life and the cat giving chase

Arnie ran like the wind, swift and fast, but barely escaping the fierce cats grasp

He jumped over logs green with moss, his hide covered in turnips, snow and frost

He tumbled through puddles and thick winter bushes but barely escaping the ginger cats' clutches!

And now in his way lay a frozen creek, forcing Arnie to halt with an almighty SCREEAACH!!!

Stuck at the shore he began to whine, trapped in a forest of snow tipped pine

Were he to cross what fate would he meet? for he hadn't feathers, a beak or webbed feet

But what choice did he have for lying in wait, was a fierce old Tom cat with an appetite to sate!

So, onto the ice he began to race, his form lacking in beauty elegance or grace!

Under his weight, the ice creaked and cracked, and Arnie wondered "should I turn back?"

But he slipped and slid, his belly in the air, with legs as stable as a newly born mare

How the Tom cat shrieked and cackled with glee, at the most amusing sight he ever did see!

But as Arnie's pace quickened, he
howled with glee and shouted to the cat
"You'll never catch me!!"

And the cats' delight did turn to despair as he
watched his supper soar through the air!

With a final push Arnie reached the shore, safe
from the Tom cat who bellowed and roared

"Bah humbug to you scrawny little hound, there's
plenty more prey in this forest to be found!"

With a final hiss he turned
and left, to search for a smaller
creature to digest!

"I'm safe at last" Arnie sighed with relief, "I'll take just a moment to rest my little feet"

But whilst he lay on the snow-covered ground, someone was spying on the frost- bitten hound

Then all of a sudden, Arnie jumped up in fear; startled by the odd rustling sound he could hear. Was it the cat come back for more? Or perhaps a vicious and hairy old boar!

With whiskers, a tail, and 3 white socks, it turned out the creature was a gorgeous young fox!

Out of the bushes she sauntered with flair, with a temper as fiery as her lovely red hair

But as luck would have it, she was also very kind, with a smile to bring peace to all of mankind

"Fear not" said she "my fine furry friend, for your fateful journey is almost at an end. You shiver and shake but you need not be alarmed; for I promise to lead you from this forest unharmed"

Taken aback, Arnie stood in awe, her radiant presence impossible to ignore.

Was she an angel sent from heaven above? To spread a Christmas message of peace and love?

Or was she a figment of Arnie's imagination; brought on by his hunger and endless starvation

To her surprise, and through no fault of his own, Arnie said to the fox (in a serious tone!)

"My beautiful lady, so fine and fair, you cannot comprehend the depths of my despair. I barely survived my most recent spat, with a mean and vicious fat ginger cat! I'm hungry and cold and so very alone; all I've ever wanted was a nice safe home. If you can help, then please lead the way, and I'll follow you, through night and day"

With a thoughtful nod and flick of her tail, she said "Follow me Arnie and you'll surely prevail!"

Not wanting to waste time, nor wither and dither, Arnie followed the fox with a renewed sense of vigour

And with his red-haired guide now by his side, he thought to himself "God bless this yule-tide!"

Together they marched along the woodland trail, past a hooting owl and squawking quail.

Over rivers cold and stinky bogs; past a herd of deer and pond full of frogs!

Through meadows and fields thick with frost, in an ancient tundra that bears once crossed!

Til finally their journey reached its end, and Arnie parted with his fateful new friend

But, before she readied herself to go, there was something she needed Arnie to know

"In this village of light and sound there live in peace, humans and hounds. Remember your manners, be courteous and kind, and a loving family I'm sure you will find".

For the kind young fox with a coat like fire, Arnie had but one question left to enquire

"Before you go my fleeting friend, and our adventure reaches its end, may I have a name to go with your face?"

To which the fox replied

"Evelyn Grace!"

Then as soon as she'd appeared, she
vanished from sight, leaving Arnie all
alone in the cold dark night

Whilst Arnie was sad to part with his friend, he
knew his venture was not at an end

And with the human town now within his sight,
Arnie left to find a home on Christmas Eve night.

And it wasn't long before into his view came
twinkling lights and festive hues!

The Christmas village was a marvellous
sight that made little Arnie
squeal in delight

A sight such as this Arnie had never seen, dazzled by colours of red blue and green

Gas fire lamps lit every street, whilst snow covered the ground Like soft cotton sheets

Holly wreaths adorned each door, and festive displays lit up every store

And in a sandstone church a choir did sing, heralding in the new born king

With all this light and cheer all around, surely somewhere there was a home to be found?

"I know what I'll do, I'll knock on each door, I'm sure there'll be a bed or at least a warm floor"

True to his word he knocked on each door, til his voice was hoarse and his paws were sore

But by time he reached number 94, it was clear his pleas would be ignored

One thing was certain for Arnie the hound; no family nor home this night would be found

He was weary and cold with nowhere to lay, no room at the inn nor manger of hay

So, with a final howl he fell to the floor, for he hadn't the will to go on anymore

Arnie had travelled many long miles, and on his journey faced no few trials.

He had managed to cross an icy creek, with a far from perfect skating technique. He had even survived a frightening attack, from a mean and viscous fat ginger cat!

But best of all, was the kindly fox, with her flaming hair and three white socks.

Yet here he lay on the cold damp ground, with no family to love nor home to be found. And as the sun rose and shone on the snow, still poor Arnie had nowhere to go

Arnie did weep a silent tear; as he felt his end would soon be near.

But wait....

What was that strange sound he could hear?
it was the sound of an engine and
it was getting very near

And was this a sleigh? No, it was a van! And who was driving but the Boston Terrier rescue man!

He ran in a hurry to the starved hound's side,
with a look of concern in his kind old eyes.

His cheeks were full and his nose bright red; with
curly brown locks adorning his head

"Please don't be scared my furry little friend, for
your troublesome journey is now at its end"

For poor little Arnie, one thing was clear;
of this dear man there was nothing to fear;
who bundled up Arnie safe in his arms,
out of the cold and safe from harm.

It was a Christmas miracle when
Arnie was found, a cold tired and
hungry little hound

But safe and warm and tucked
up in bed Arnie could finally
rest his weary head

That night he dreamed of the woodland trail,
the hooting owl and squawking quail.
The stinking bog and pond of frogs,
in the ancient tundra that bears
once crossed.

He'd always be grateful to Evelyn Grace;
who'd helped him find this
warm happy place.

And the good tidings continued for
Arnie the hound, for a loving home
had now been found!

Arnie had found his happy ever after; with promises of joy, fun and laughter

And with five older siblings, a cousin or two, he knew with this family he could never be blue.

And how dear little Arnie sobbed and wept, safe in the arms of his new mummy Beth

So, this festive season with joy all around please spare a thought for poor abandoned hounds

Who will spend their day in the cold outside with nothing but their will to help them survive

So, I shall I leave you with a final thought; to remember the lessons this story has taught

Now as the moon rises and heralds the night, I wish you all a merry Christmas, and I bid you goodnight.

Printed in Great Britain
by Amazon